Calico City

And The Darkest Hour

Rosalie Mussig

 pencil

ISBN 978-93-5667-107-2
© Rosalie Mussig 2022
Published in India 2022 by Pencil

A brand of
One Point Six Technologies Pvt. Ltd.
123, Building J2, Shram Seva Premises,
Wadala Truck Terminal, Wadala (E)
Mumbai 400037, Maharashtra, INDIA
E connect@thepencilapp.com
W www.thepencilapp.com

Author biography

Hello, my name is Rosalie! This book was an inspiration off of a game me and my sister made up. I thought it was interesting, so I began writing, and now, it will become a series! I love animals, and writing. I am 11 years old! I am also from Ohio. I hope that this book interests you, and you enjoy!

CONTENTS

Acknowledgements

Come read the next book:
Calico City: The Next Gen.
For an adventure packed journey!

Introduction

A dog named Mercury is dropped off at the Calico City Animal Shelter and Pound from his owners after he attacked them because they had abused him. In this action-filled adventure, Mercury makes some friends at the shelter and eventually finds out about the cats. He starts to attempt to find ways to get into the cat area, although they will punish the dogs unremorsefully for attacking cats, maybe even leading to being put down. Mercury eventually ends up getting to a cat named Negro, almost killing him. Mercury is sent to the chamber and eventually escapes into the wilderness, finally being brought back to the "Pound" and locked in a cage. The people at Calico City Animal Shelter and Pound damaged the dogs and treat cats like royalty, giving them everything. Everyone who lives in Calico City owns a cat, dogs are technically illegal to own without a permit, with them being damaged or called monsters. The animals work together to change this, leading to the change of Calico City to bring back the long-gone city of Wilderness City, to accept and bring back the loving of animals, to bring back the loved ones who were lost inside, the strays will be no more. Animals are returning, and Jasper will .

CHARACTERS:

Dogs   Wolf-Dogs

1) Tokyo (German Shepard)   1) Tsunami.
(Samoyed/German Shepard + Arctic wolf)
2) Saturn (Husky)   2) Syko (Arctic Wolf +
    Samoyed)
3) Mercury (Samoyed)   3) Tolo (Mexican wolf +
German Shepard)
4) Venus (Golden Retriever)
5) Pluto (Husky + German Shepard)
6) Miko (Goberian)
7) Amari (Husky)
8) Dodge (Husky)
9) Fluffy (Pomeranian)
10) Runner (Chihuahua)
11) Niro (Australian Shepard)
12) Rico (White Swiss Shepard Dog)

Cats

1) Negro   13) Neko
2) Silky   14) Siro
3) Milky
4) Pine
5) Moca
6) Shadow
7) Creme
8) Sweety
9) Quail

10) Flair
11) Kiko
12) Kyro

Mercury

"Grrr!" Mercury growled at his owners as they held up a shoe in front of his face and a chain in the other hand, backing him up into a corner. Mercury jumps onto his owners, unremorsefully attacking their faces. His owners fell to the ground while holding their hands over their faces, doing so, they ended up dropping the chains and shoes. Mercury sprinted out of the doggy door, running out into the street. "Gah.." Mercury groaned, now limping on his paw. "My paw! It hurts," Mercury whined, limping to the other side of the street and then laying down in a tunnel in the mountain across the road. "Geez, it's dark in here," Mercury said. "SCREEE" bats screeched then flew out of the cave in an abundance. "GAHH" Mercury yelled, then sprinting out. Mercury eventually ran back home, as it was too cold outside for him to be roaming the streets. When Mercury got home, he saw his owners putting all his stuff in the trunk. "Get in you dumb mutt!" Juniper screamed. Mercury jumped in, not wanting to get hit by his owners. When they reached their destination, Juniper opened the car door and yanked Mercury out. "Hey!-.." Mercury whined, just then, they pulled a shock collar over his head. "If you don't listen, we will shock you with this, got that?" Juniper yelled, as her voice echoed through the air. Mercury whined. Then Juniper began to start walking, tugging Mercury around the parking lot, through the large spinning doors to the shelter. Out of nowhere, she began to cry, but Mercury knew that wasn't any crying, that was her acting cry. Mercury groaned, then felt a stinging on his neck. Juniper turned the shock collar on! He whined, the shocking, it was painful. Mercury's fur bristled at the stinging. Mercury began to listen, limping his way inside wherever they were. Just then, the next thing he knew, his owners were at a desk talking to someone. "Yes, he is belligerent. I had bent down to pet him and he bit me!" Juniper shouted, but Mercury knew she was lying. "Alright then, we will take him to the pound section; he will have 20 days to get out of here before we put him down." The receptionist said. "20 days!? Wait.. the POUND!?" Mercury thought to himself. Mercury began to whine, just then, his "owner" turned the shock collar to the highest level, making Mercury's eyes fill with tears. As he sat there in pain, his "owners" continued to speak with the receptionist of the Calico City Animal Shelter and Pound. Mercury was in pain, but knew he couldn't do anything. But then, his "owners" sat his leash down on the counter and began walking to the door, nodding to the receptionist from the front desk.

Pound

Mercury then saw his ex-owners walk out as the guard of the pound grabbed his chained leash and tugged him through the "shelter" then bringing the white, and fluffy samoyed to this wet and mucky cage. He yanked the chained leash off and grabbed the shock collar's controller, then threw the dog into the cage, slid a bowl of water and food under the cage door, and yelled, "Muts. So annoying." Mercury pinned his ears, terrified, and then looked over to see a mucky, dark-colored, short-furred, tall-eared, large dog laying down in his cage with his ears pinned and his eyes half-closed. "Hey, are you okay?" Mercury asked. Then, the large dog burst into the air, realizing someone was talking to him. "Yes, I am fine." the dog said. "You sure?" Mercury said. "Yes, i'm sure." the dog said, "My name is Mercury, how about you?" Mercury said, lifting his tail, wagging it. "I'm Tokyo, nice to meet you," Tokyo said. "Nice to meet you too!" Mercury barked, then spun around in a circle and then grabbed his tail, stopping, and then letting it go. "How long have you been here?" Mercury asked, "I've been here for maybe 2 months?" Tokyo responded. "Wow.. that is a long time. I only have 20 days here before they put me down." Mercury said. "Only 20 days? That only happens to aggressive dogs who get dropped off here!" Tokyo barked. "Well, my owners hit me, so I bit their face before they hurt me again," Mercury said. "But you didn't do it to be aggressive, you did it for self-defense, what did they say? Did they lie about you?" Tokyo snarled. "Yeah, kinda," Mercury said, wrapping his tail around is now-muddy paws. "These cages are uncomfortable and gross," Mercury said. "How do you think I feel?" Tokyo said, then shaking his wet and nasty fur everywhere, making water fly through the air and splash Mercury in the face. "Gah!" Mercury barked, squinting his eyes. "Now my fur is all muddy!" Mercury shouted. "Shhh! They are coming! Act natural!" Tokyo shouted, laying down to sleep. "Huh?" Mercury didn't understand so he didn't listen. The guard of the pound came around, looking around at all the dogs. Some dogs barked and others whined. The owner of the place hit the cages with a chain, silencing the loud dogs. Mercury, however, sat there whining, not sure what was going on. Tokyo was eyeing Mercury, panting nervously. The owner came around and finally lay his eyes on Mercury, and grinned. The owner opened the cage and stook his hand through the collar, dragging Mercury out of the cage, and hit him with a chain, leaving a bloody mess on his face. Mercury escaped his grip and ran back into the cage, whimpering. The large dog was in pain, licking the blood off his face. He layd down and put his paws over his face and his tail beneath is hind legs. The owner then walked away, further up the hall of cages. It was now silent in the pound, not a noise could be heard. Just then, as the guard walked off, Tokyo sat up and looked Merucry in the eye.

Tokyo

Tokyo knew how Mercury felt. His owners, also, hadn't been the nicest. He wasn't sure if it was just because they were stressed about work or something. Tokyo did a lot of work for his "owners", like running, fetching, training, sniffing, and finding, but that might've just been because he was a police dog in training. *I guess* he didn't do enough work for them and that is why they dumped him in the pound. Although, they were upset when they did it. Tokyo wasn't 100% sure if he was accurate or not, but all he knew is his "owners" gave him up and they weren't coming back. That is that. Tokyo felt a pain in his chest like he had eaten something bad. The next thing he knew, he was gagging and sitting up. Had he *blacked out*for a moment? He wasn't sure. All he knew is that he was about to - "LGhauwa." "Ewwww," Mercury said. Tokyo pinned his ears, looking at the pile of muck. *What just happened? he thought to himself.* Am I *sick?* Tokyo thought to himself. No, I can't be. Tokyo stood up and then spun around once, and laid down in his bed. A guard came around and cleaned up the pile of muck, *scolding* Tokyo. Tokyo whined in annoyance. "Mph.." Tokyo mumbled. Tokyo then fell asleep and rested until morning.

In the morning, Tokyo was awoken by a small dog screeching his name. "Tokyo! Tokyo!" Runner, the chihuahua screeched, wagging his tail, eccentrically. "Come on, come on!" Runner screeched again. "Yes, Runner," Tokyo yawned, lifting his head up. "Time for training!" Runner barked. "Alright.. coming," Tokyo responded. Tokyo stood up and followed Runner to the training room, where they had sat down in front of a large screen. "ugh, I hate this so much. Can we go back now?" Mercury complained the moment he sat down. One of the trainers at the pound came into the room and stood in front of the screen. As the trainer stood in front of the screen, Tokyo looked upward and saw a bird fly over the sky roof. Tokyo then felt sad, remembering his "owners". He pinned his ears and tucked his tail under him and then howled, making all the dogs in the room set off. Tokyo then stopped, and set a paw over his muzzle, closed his eyes, and lowered his head as he listened to the dogs stop and listen to the orders of the trainer to be quiet.

Training

Once all the dogs were quiet and the trainer was ready to start, the trainer spoke. The trainer was very loud, not to mention the echo, when the trainer spoke, they said, "Our dogs, today, will be racing. You will each get a number and find your place on the track. Once everyone has reached the track, we will start the race with a countdown. To win, you must go around the 3-mile long track 5 times, the winner receives a treat basket, wet food, fancy dog food, a cleaned cage, a groom, and a new bed, water bowl, and food bowl."

After the trainer passed out the numbers, the dogs looked down and walked over to their place on the track. When they all got onto the track, a countdown was above their head. "10, 9, 8, 7, 6, 5, 4, 3, 2, 1," and off they went. Racing around the track like cheetahs! Mercury was far behind, not able to catch up with the others dogs with his tired legs. He sat down for a moment, panting. He wondered, where is the water? Just then, Mercury sniffed the air and scented water not too far ahead. Mercury stood up and ran as fast as he could to the water, he was panting heavily. Once he finally reached the water station, he drank the bowl of water quickly. Suddenly, he felt a bolt of energy strike through his body, and he sprinted off, running *faster than a cheetah*. Mercury eventually caught up with the other dogs, almost passing first place, Runner. Runner, the chihuahua. "How are you, YOU in FIRST place?" Mercury asked Runner, "Well, I may be tiny, but my legs are filled with energy." Runner responded to the large, fluffy white Samoyed. Out of nowhere, Mercury sprinted, moving his legs even faster, making sharp turns. What was going on? he thought. Just then, he looked back and saw all the dogs surprised, and himself, way ahead of the other dogs. He realized that he had gone around the track about two times already. Only a couple more times to win! Mercury thought, but then, Tokyo sped up and passed him. "Cya!" he shouted to Mercury as he sprinted quickly around the track. Mercury began to slow down, tired. He pinned his ears and walked off to the side of the track, sat down, and started panting. Mercury turned to see a puddle under a large pine tree in the large training room. He walked over and drank some of the water, thirstily. Runner, Fluffy, Miko, Rico, Saturn, Venus, Pluto, Dodge, Amari, and Niro all passed by him, racing down the track, and then looked at him and gave him a rude look. Mercury felt sad. Why can't he fit in? He thought. Then shaking the water out of his fur. Knowing he wasn't going to win the race, he still got back onto the track and attempted to run as fast as before. After he had gone around the track about 4 times, he was finally about to be next to Tokyo, who was still in first. He tried running faster and faster, as quick as he could and eventually reached the point where he was right next to Tokyo. They made one last turn, and half a mile ahead was the finish line. "Mercury is now in, and Tokyo passes him, taking the lead! Mercury doesn't let that stop him, and sprints up ahead and takes 1st place! Who will win? And oh! Tokyo Takes the lead once again, barking at

Mercury!" He heard in the air, ringing through his ear. "Ugh," Tokyo complained. "And who will win? They have reached 200 feet before any dog steps paw over the line!" Announcements shouted. Mercury sprinted even faster, now passing up Tokyo. He was about 50 feet away now, and, "Tokyo wins!" Announcements shouted, echoing through the massive training room. "WHAT!?" Mercury shouted, then saw Tokyo over the finish line, panting, in a winning stance. How? He thought, then seeing Tokyo's paw prints on the marbled walls. He ran on the walls? Mercury thought.

The Cats

After the race, the dogs were dismissed to their cages and Tokyo was receiving his prize(s). Mercury's legs had begun to hurt, badly. Mercury walked slowly to his cage, with his ears pinned, eyes half-closed, head down, and tail in a timid position. As he finally reached his cage, he lay down and immediately fell asleep.

A few hours later, he awoke to a strange noise. "MeoWWW," A cat called, "What was that?" Mercury yelled, lifting himself off the ground, his tail begginning to wag with curiosity. Then, a small cat, black, walked up to his cage and rubbed itself against it. "CAT! CAT! CAT!" Mercury shouted, now wagging his tail uncontrollably. He spun around, acting like a crazy schizophrenic. He clawed and smacked at his cage. Out! Out! He thought. Then, the cat stepped a few steps away from the cage. "Chill out, mangy mutt. My name is Negro, what about you?" Negro said, "I'm Mercury. Why don't you just let me out now," Mercury said, trying to play the cat. "I'd prefer not to. I know your intentions." Negro responded, rubbing herself against a wall. "Well now, if I must, I will be heading to the cat's room. Cya, dog." Negro said, walking off, waving her tail in the air, then crawling through a hole. "Cat area?" Mercury said, "Wait, an area full of cats!" Mercury said, "Yes, yes, yes!" Mercury shouted, awakening all of the dogs. "Oops," Mercury said, guilty. "Heh."

A few hours later, Mercury was still staring out of his cage, trying to think of a way to escape, but then, he saw the latch and climbed up his cage and then unlatched it by poking his claw through the cage . "That was easy," he said. He pushed open the cage door and stepped out into the opening of the hallway, and looked around for the hole in the wall. He looked over and saw it, he ran over to the hole and stuck his head through, seeing a pitch-black hallway in the hole. He attempted to fit himself into the tunnel, although it was a very small tunnel. All the walls were touching him. He pushed himself through the hole, and eventually reached the other side and found himself in the room of cats. He looked and his tail started to wag and drool fell from his mouth, he then began running around the cat area, known as Cat Crazy Exhibit; his eyes then settled on one cat.

Negro

Negro was relaxing when he noticed a large dog running toward him. He recognized the dog from earlier, he was in the Dirty Dogs Exhibit. Negro sighed, and then called out somebodies name. "Tsunami!" Negro shouted. Just then, a large and buffy wolf-dog trotted out of a small den in the corner of the exhibit. He trotted over and saw the small Samoyed dog, and began to speak. "How dare you attempt to hurt my cats?" The wolf-dog questioned, with a disgusted look on his face. "I- I just wanted to see a cat?.." Mercury pinned his ears and began panting. "Heheh...?" Mercury said, beginning to get worried about what this wolf-dog could do to him. He was massive, a large creature. Not a very nice one either. Although, Mercury probably isn't the nicest either he thought to himself. "Well uh, I'll be going-" Mercury shouted, sprinting off to the door, but then, he switched around and hit behind a corner. "Hah." He whispered. Tsunami walked off and went back to his den. Then, Mercury sprinted out, grabbed negro by the neck, threw her down, bit off half her tail, as well as half an ear, clawed one of her eyes, and took one of her legs. Negro cried for help, terrified. Her body was shaking, once Mercury realized what he had done, he sprinted off to the Dirty Dog Exhibit. Tsunami sprinted out of his den and ran to Negro. He picked her up off the ground and licked her wounds. Tsunami sprinted over to the guards and set her down. The guards immediately rushed the cat over to the Hospital Home For Dogs and Cats, aka the animal hospital, and talked to one of the "vets" more known as veterinarians. The veterinarian lay the she-cat down and pet her fur as they gave her a shot to put her to sleep. The veterinarian lay bandages on her neck wound, so the bleeding could stop. She wrapped the end of her tail in bandages, as well as her leg. She covered the wounds on her in bandages, and put a small bandage on her ear. She placed a patch over Negro's eye, and let Negro sleep in the sleeping room. She lay Negro down in one of the beds, and put a glass barrier around the bed to provide oxygen while she slept.

A few hours later, DNA tests came back to see who's fur was in between her claws. As expected, Mercurys DNA matched up with the DNA in between her claws. Mercury later, saw a man walk up to his cage and drag him by his collar, and then threw him into the chamber as punishment for his actions.

Broken Chambers

When Mercury lay there in the chamber, he heard some muttering voices from behind the walls. It was hot in here, Mercury thought, beggining to pant. He looked around, his vision was getting blurry. He saw a window, and he attempted climbing the walls to reach it. When he got close to the window, he went to hang onto the latch on it, to pull himself up, but all it did was knock him down and open the window. When Mercury saw that the window was open, he had an idea. "What if I just leave, and become a stray? I don't want to be locked inside a cage my whole life." Mercury said. Mercury began climbing the wall of the chamber, and finally reached the window. He pushed himself out and jumped out the ledge of the window and landed on the ground. "I'm free!" He barked happily. Then he remembered his friends. He felt sad for a moment but then thought, they never cared, they were only here for the rewards. Mercury sprinted off and ran over the street into the pitch black forest, where he had dug a hole in the ground to make himself a den. He was happy, he felt free, relieved, and tired. He lay himself down to sleep and then he heard a loud noise.

Mercury lifted himself up, stretched his back and legs, and climbed out of the decent sized den. He looked to his right and saw a light, fluffy, white dog, covered in mud. He walked up to the strange animal, and placed a paw in front of him. The small white, and fluffy animal sniffed his pelt. He turned red. The female animal rubbed her head onto his neck and then sprinted off, stopped for a moment, looked back, pinned her ears, and then went on her way again. "Wait!-" Mercury shouted, but it was too late. She was already gone, and out of sight. Mercury climbed back into his den, and went back to bed. His eyes fluttered in his sleep, dreaming about the strange looking, but beautiful creature he had just seen in the woods. His shiny, but mudded pelt glinted in the moonlight, before he knew it, it was finally daytime.

Mysterious Creature

The next morning when Mercury woke up, he heard the same rustling noise from before. He climbed out of his den once again and saw the same female animal, pawing at a bush of berries. Once again, he walked over to the female animal, and this time, she looked at him wither her *dark amber eyes.* Mercury turned pink like a pig and pinned his ears down. The female then said something, "Hello." Mercury paused, and he lifted his ears. "Hey." He said. "My name is Syko, I'm a wolf dog. How about you?" Syko said. "Uh... I'm Mercury- and I'm a Uhm... Samoyed?" Mercury stuttered. "I love Samoyeds," Syko said. "You do!?- I- I mean, of course, you do. Everyone likes Samoyeds." Mercury said, stuttering, once more. Mercury was blushing so hard, he didn't know what to say. He was "in love". Mercury asked, "Want to see my den?" and then Syko responded, "Sure." Both of the animals walked over to the paw-dug den, and walked down into it. It was a medium-sized den, big enough to fit 2-3 full-grown adult wolves, and maybe 5-6 pups. "It's nice," Syko blushed a bit. Just then. Mercury heard rustling, he jumped out of his den and saw two of the guards from the shelter coming into the forest. Mercury told Syko to run, which she did. She looked back and saw the people grab Mercury by the throat with a net, and he made choking noises. They hooked a chain leash to him and tazed him. He whined in agony. Syko ran over and bit the people's legs. They tripped, and Mercury jumped out of their arms, but his chain leash was in someones hands. The person who fell called for backup and more guards came. They managed to grab both Mercury and Syko, and there they were, now sitting in cages at the shelter, once again. Syko glanced around, frightened at the sudden cramped space. Her eyes shut in fear, and her fur bristled. She let out a spine tingling howl before falling to the ground and tucking her tail beneath her legs.

Punishment

Mercury paced back and forth, silently waiting as echoing footsteps came to the air. The people who were walking toward the cages were holding Syko by the collar, her claws were scraping against the ground as she was attempting to sit as she slid across the floor. They dragged her and threw her in the cage across from him. She whined a bit, and Mercury whispered to her. "Hey, are you okay?" She responded, shaking. "Yeah." Mercury stepped back, now hearing footsteps again, layed down, and then silently pinned his ears and closed his eyes. The people came to the cages, and Mercury stood up and he heard a leash click. They opened his cage and put him on the leash, now walking him to the training room and taking him to a big box in the corner of the room. They threw him in, with food and water, and then shut and locked the door. They then put the heat in the room to 100° and left the training room, leaving him by himself in the hot room. He panted, and his vision was blurry. He heard the smacking on cages and the whining of puppies and dogs. Elder dogs cried, feeling sick and unhealthy. Tokyo was most likely avoided, as Mercury didn't hear his bark or whine, all because he won the contest. Mercury was annoyed and hot. Now scratching at the door and walls, and eventually, finding his way out through a hole in the wall. He ran through the training room and out the door into the air conditioned

Dirty Dog room, where he smuggled himself back into his cage, where he layed down and chugged his water. He looked across the hallway to the other cage, and Syko was laying there, looking upset, or sick. The guards paused at her cage, staring at the upset, now-dirty "dog" then walked away, carelessly.

Syko

Syko was whining, not feeling well. She lifted her head to see Mercury staring at her. She coughed, then whined once again as she felt a pain, and then a weird tickle in her stomach. She stood up, startled of the feeling, and kept feeling it. The guards noticed her strange behavior and brought her to the examination room, where they did x-rays and treatments. As they did an ultra-sound, they spotted emroiyds inside her, meaning she was pregnant! They did a DNA sample on Mercury, as he was the one they found her with, and of course, it popped up as positive for the father of the pups. The guards were shocked, not even angry. These would be some rare puppies, and they could get a lot for them. Syko was then brought to a bigger cage with a box inside, and Mercury was placed in the cage with her. It was a strange scent for Mercury. He'd never smelt something like this before. He layed down next to Syko, and Syko layed with him willingly, as she relaxed her muscles and fell asleep. She dreamt about the stars and the moon and both of them being free and running through the forest. She pictured the pups playing in the dirt and having a fun, and free life. Her breathing was steady, and she continued to dream.

When Syko woke up, she heard loud banging noises, and her startled self jumped upwards. She was terrified by the sounds. Syko widened her eyes as she saw a guard banging a chain in the cages, yelling at a the dogs to wake up. It was time for the dogs and cats to go face to face. Syko had a bad feeling about this, knowing Mercury's sudden instinct when he notices a cat. She gulped, and her stomach dropped.

The Meeting of Cats

Mercury paused, his tail now wagging in excitement as he padded outward of his cage, keeping his back straight and his legs tall. He spread a smile across his face before sitting down at the meeting spot. Then, the cats were released. They paced around gracefully and menacingly, while staring at the drooling dogs. Mercury couldn't handle himself anymore, and before they knew it, "CATS!" he'd scream, chasing and running after them all. The other dogs barked in a warning at Mercury, and before he knew it, Mercury was being chased by Tsunami. "Uh oh- he's soooo done for." Saturn squealed. "Yep." Tokyo agreed. The guards were also chasing after Mercury, holding their tasers. Tsunami grabbed Mercury's tail, finally caught up, as the cats scattered around the room, shaking. He yelped in pain, feeling b the strong rug of his tail and turned around, biting Tsunamis face roughly, dragging his teeth across his eye. Tsunami let out a loud whine of pain before trampling over his paws to the ground, blood dripping from his face. He laid down as Mercury skidded to a stop, backing up slowly as guards surrounded him. They caught him, now dragging him through the feild to the list, an odd list. And wrote his name down as 6. They lifted him off the ground by his collar, and showed him the list. "14, you're 14 days in. 6 days until your execution, pup." The guard spoke. The other dogs gasped in disbelief, before lowering their heads.

Mercury was terrified, now sitting in his cage, feeling a rumble of his stomach. His paws were spread atleast a foot away from eachother, and his tail was tucked. His eyes were shortened and his ears were lowered. He felt as guilty as ever. He shot back his memories to when he lived happily with his owners, watching TV on the couch and reading stories or eating snacks. When everyone was happy. But when they had their baby, everything changed, all of that happiness disappeared. Like none of it ever happened. He was hit all the time and called bad dog. Was I a bag dog? The flashback suddenly disappeared to the voice of an unrecognized person.

Jasper

Jasper was a girl who had always wanted pets. She had finally raised enough to get one. So she decided to rescue a dog from the Calico City Animal Shelter. She began walking, since it was so close by. Once she arrived, she came to the front desk, explaining herself. They then escorted her to the back where they introduced her to the animals. Her eyes widened, as she looked at all the animals with despair and sadness. Her fingers dragged along the cages, glancing at all the animals, finally choosing three of interest. Known as, Name: Fluffy Breed: Pomeranian Age: 5 months Time kept - three months. Name: Tokyo Breed: German Shepard Age: 8 years Time kept: 3 years Service time: Police dog, 4 years. And lastly, Name: Negro Breed: Bombay Age: 3 years Time kept: 1 year. Jasper looked happy, filing out the forms of identification, and the for a License to own a dog. (Dogs). Jasper smiled as she left the pound with her new pets, placing their cages in the trunk. Mercury, inside the pound looked over after awakening from his nap to see that Tokyo was gone. He looked around, not seeing him anywhere. "Where's Tokyo?" Mercury stated, asking a question. "Oh, he was adopted.." Saturn spoke, responding to Mercury. "What?" Mercury lowered his head. "It can't be.."

Jasper kicked open the door, releasing the animals from

their cages for then to explore their new home and to get used to the new scents and change of habitat. The animals sprinted around, excitedly playing inside the massive home, and making themselves at home in which it seemed minutes. Jasper giggled at the playful Animals, then walking to the kitchen to cook some food.

The People

Calico City is a place where cats are treated like royalty, and dogs are treated like a nasty monster. But now, it will change. The people of Calico City gathered in the town square foe a new election of a mayor. Animals and all. It was time that someone who accepted all animals to rule the city and change all of the hate that these humans could possibly give. Mercury glanced around in the new area, then seeing his old owners, he looked back to his paws. "Welcome everybody to the Election of our new Mayor, we have thought long and hard about the decision we've finally made, and have decided to Name our new mayor, Jasper!" The now-previous mayor spoke. Jasper howled in excitement before trotting up to the microphone. "Thank you, thank you everybody! Really! I'm very excited to be able to take on this position as mayor, and bring the now dark times of Calico City to light, and bring home our Wilderness city! This moment brings me so much joy, and I thank you all for allowing it to happen. So as the new mayor of Calico City, I declare all animals welcome and treated fairly, and the name of this city to now go and be known as.. Wilderness City!" Jasper called, boldly from the stage. Letting out a howl of love toward the dogs in the van. Suddenly, all of the animals were released from the cages into the crowd where they were welcomed by the citizens of Wilderness City in their arms, and Mercury, he was still lowering his head in the side walk, but was suddenly greeted with the warmth of his old owners arms, and dreadful treats falling to his pelt, and Syko, well, her and her pups were greeted to. And Mercury found himself in a loving home once again, and was soon to be greeted to his friends again.

9 789356 671072